First published in Great Britain 2020 by Red Shed,
an imprint of Egmont UK Limited
Egmont UK Limited, 2 Minster Court, 10th Floor, London EC3R 7BB

www.egmont.co.uk

Text copyright © Catherine Barr 2020
Illustrations copyright © Yuliya Gwilym 2020

ISBN 978 1 4052 9256 6

Consultancy by Dr Helen Czerski.

A CIP catalogue record for this title is available from the British Library.

Stay safe online. Egmont is not responsible for content hosted by third parties.

Egmont takes its responsibility to the planet and its inhabitants very seriously.
We aim to use papers from well-managed forests run by responsible suppliers.

# HOW COLOUR WORKS

Written by
## Catherine Barr

Illustrated by
## Yuliya Gwilym

RED SHED

# Into the rainbow

Colour comes from light, which speeds
forwards until it hits something. Then
it bends, bounces back or sinks in.
This movement of light helps
create the colours
that we see.

When sunlight shines on raindrops,
the light bends and splits. We see different
colours — a rainbow — arc across the sky.

Light travels in waves. Some light waves are short and bouncy,
while others are longer and flatter. Every colour has its own wavelength.

If the wavelength of light is long, we see red.

If the light waves are medium, we see green.

If the light waves are short, we see violet.

**From green grass to blue sky, pink
pigs and yellow flowers, our planet is
flooded with colour. Follow the rainbow
to discover how colour really works . . .**

# Creating colour

Light waves sink into or bounce off tiny parts called pigments. These are found in plants, animals and non-living things. Different types of pigment make different colours.

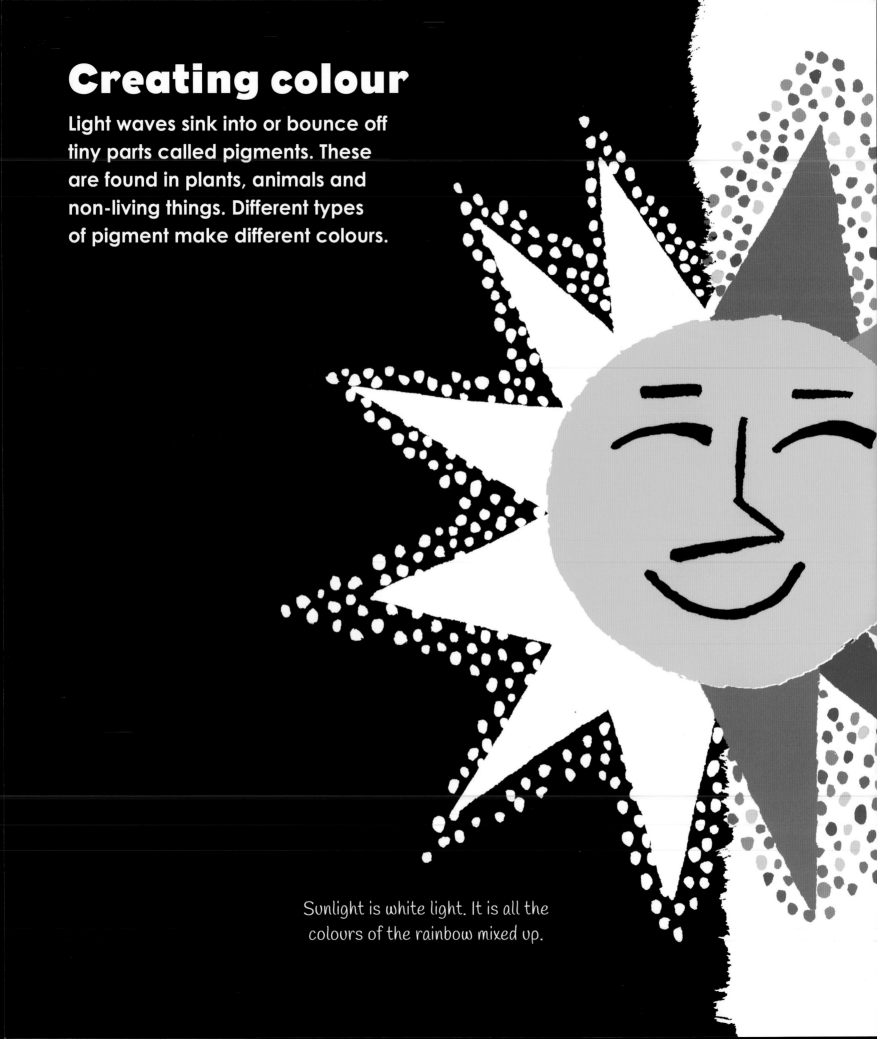

Sunlight is white light. It is all the colours of the rainbow mixed up.

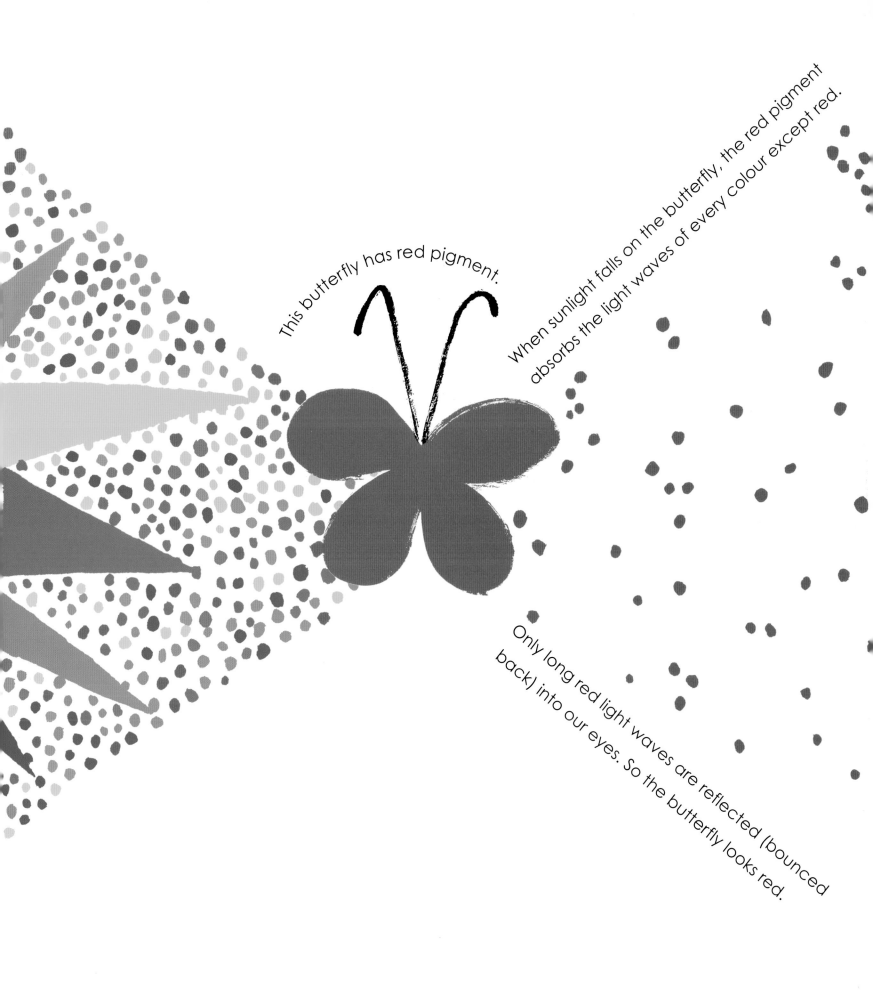

This butterfly has red pigment.

When sunlight falls on the butterfly, the red pigment absorbs the light waves of every colour except red.

Only long red light waves are reflected (bounced back) into our eyes. So the butterfly looks red.

# How eyes work

Nothing in the world really has its own colour. Colour is made inside our heads. Our eyes collect light, then our brain tells us which colours we are looking at.

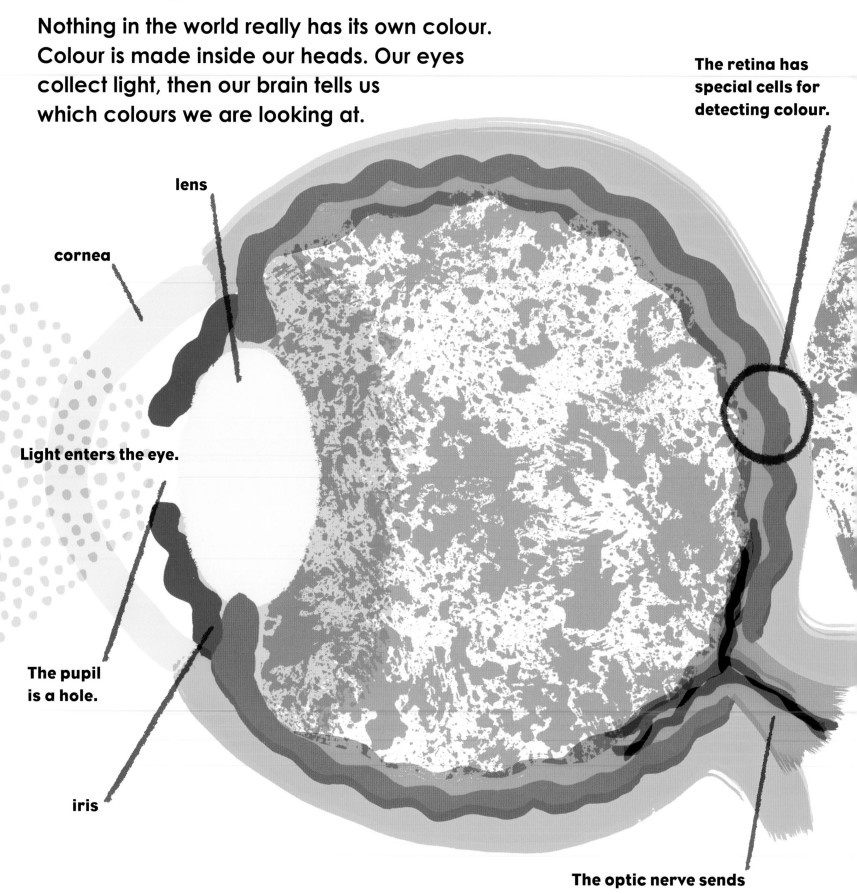

The retina has special cells for detecting colour.

lens

cornea

Light enters the eye.

The pupil is a hole.

iris

The optic nerve sends messages to the brain.

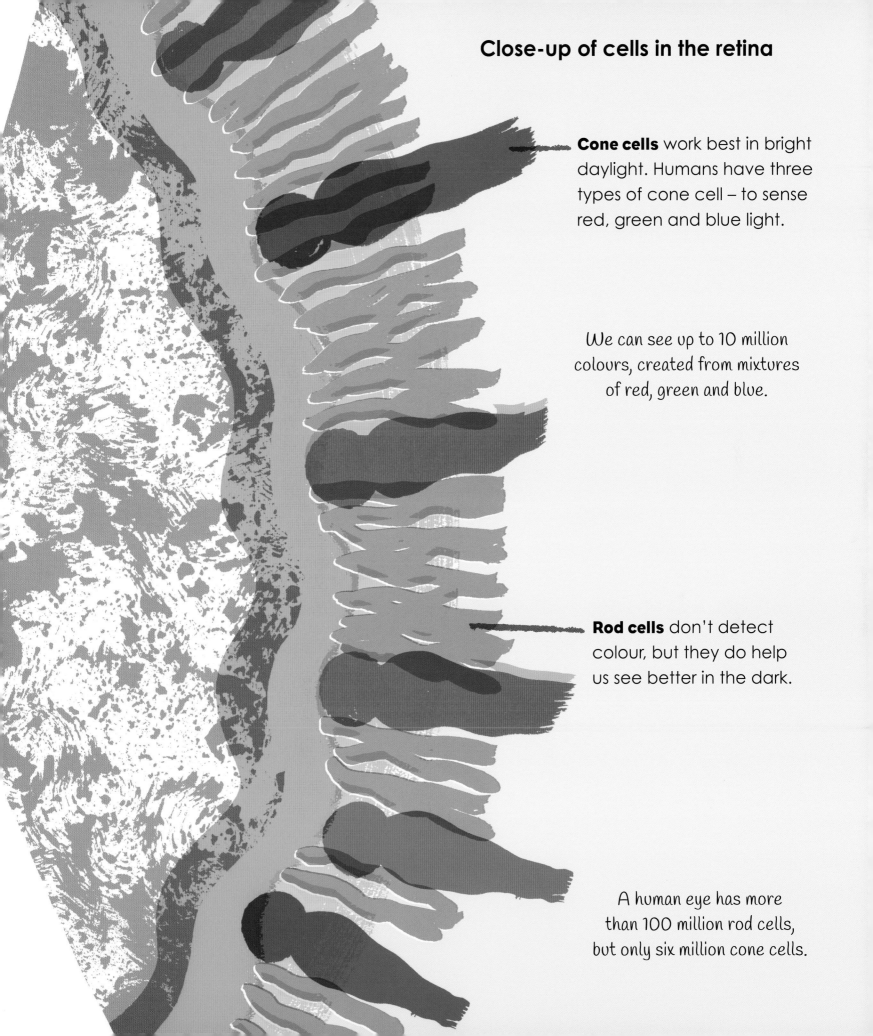

# Close-up of cells in the retina

**Cone cells** work best in bright daylight. Humans have three types of cone cell – to sense red, green and blue light.

We can see up to 10 million colours, created from mixtures of red, green and blue.

**Rod cells** don't detect colour, but they do help us see better in the dark.

A human eye has more than 100 million rod cells, but only six million cone cells.

# Seeing colour

We will never know exactly what each animal sees when it opens its eyes. But by learning about different types of eyes, we can imagine.

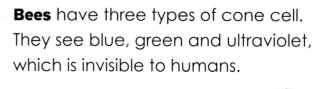

**Bees** have three types of cone cell. They see blue, green and ultraviolet, which is invisible to humans.

**Dogs** see everything in shades of blue, yellow, grey and sludgy brown. They have only yellow and blue cone cells – so they cannot see red or bright green.

Ultraviolet may look bright violet to bees. Ultraviolet patterns on petals guide bees to nectar.

**Pigeons** have at least four types of cone cell. They eye up a dazzling kaleidoscope of colour.

**Snails** look at a blurry black-and-white world. With eye spots on the tips of their tentacles, they see fuzzy shapes and grey shades.

When a pigeon looks at grass, it probably sees green in shades invisible to the human eye.

# Sky blue

Air is mostly made of two gases: oxygen and nitrogen. Most light waves pass straight through them. But blue light bounces and scatters, painting the sky a beautiful blue.

Water absorbs red and green light. Only the blue light is left, so the ocean looks blue.

The skin of a **blue whale** is
actually grey, but it reflects
the bright blue of the ocean.

# Talking in colour

Animals use colour to send messages. These pinks, blues and yellows scare predators, impress mates or tell others they're here to help.

**Male mandrills** have bright faces and bottoms to attract females. Their colourful behinds might also help these monkeys follow each other through thick forest.

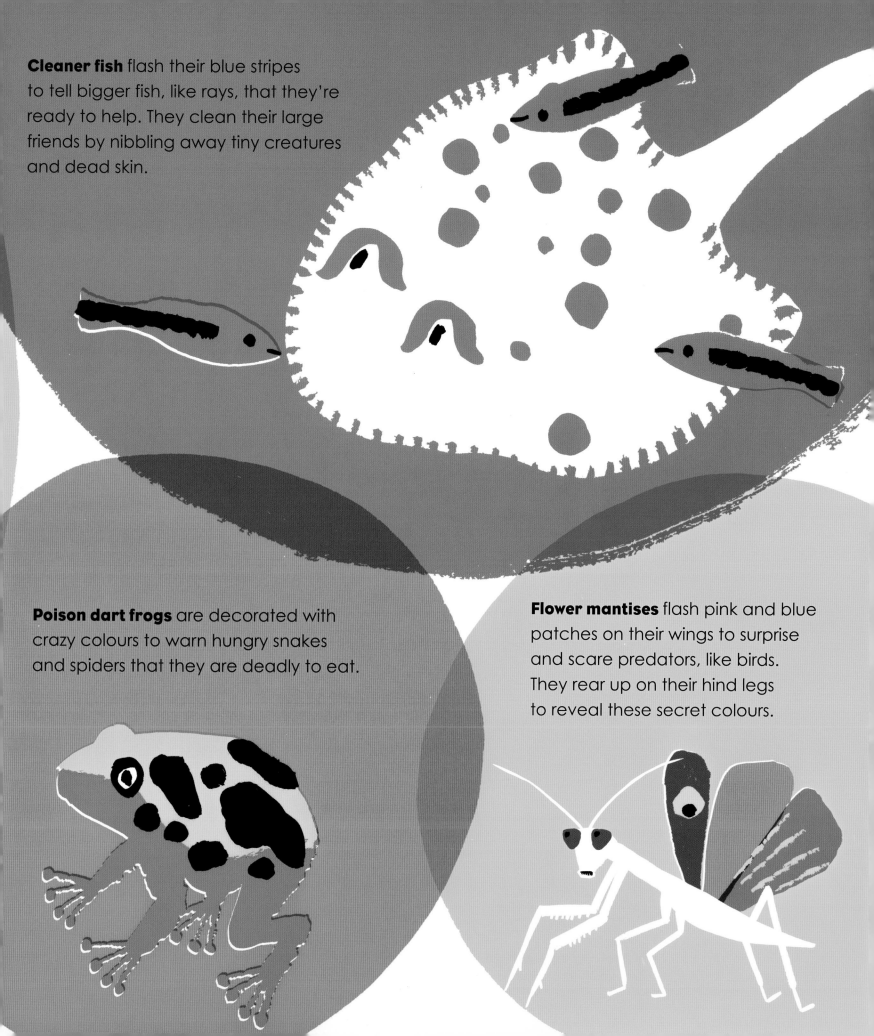

**Cleaner fish** flash their blue stripes to tell bigger fish, like rays, that they're ready to help. They clean their large friends by nibbling away tiny creatures and dead skin.

**Poison dart frogs** are decorated with crazy colours to warn hungry snakes and spiders that they are deadly to eat.

**Flower mantises** flash pink and blue patches on their wings to surprise and scare predators, like birds. They rear up on their hind legs to reveal these secret colours.

# Snow white

When sunlight hits the shiny
ice crystals packed inside snow,
it bounces back. Sunlight is
white light – so snow looks white.

In winter, the fur of the **Arctic fox**
loses its dark pigment and grows
clear. It then reflects white sunlight,
perfect for camouflage in the snow.

The dark pigment in the fox's
nose absorbs all sunlight,
making it look black.

# Changing colours

Some animals change the colours of their skin for camouflage, to send a message or just to keep warm. Others use tricks of light to make their colours shimmer and shine.

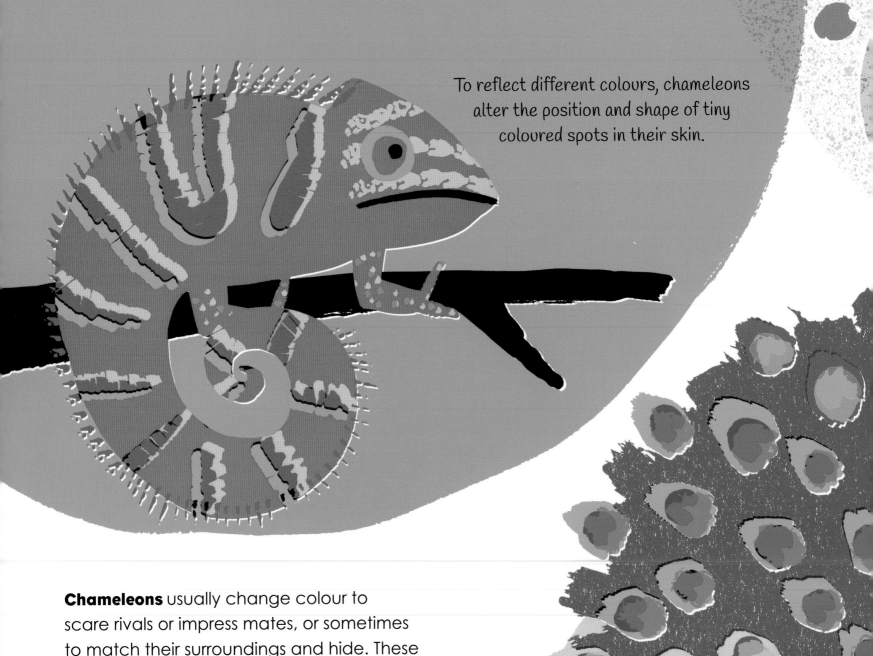

To reflect different colours, chameleons alter the position and shape of tiny coloured spots in their skin.

**Chameleons** usually change colour to scare rivals or impress mates, or sometimes to match their surroundings and hide. These cold-blooded lizards can even darken their skin to absorb more of the Sun's warming rays.

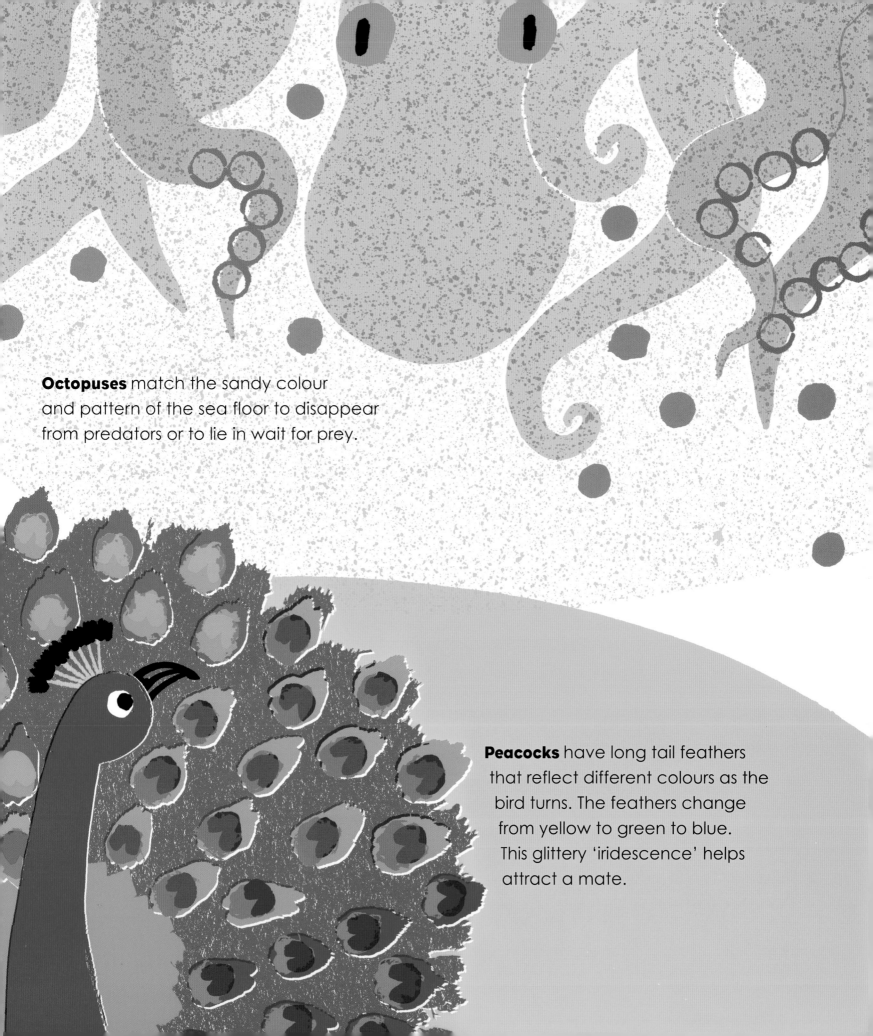

**Octopuses** match the sandy colour and pattern of the sea floor to disappear from predators or to lie in wait for prey.

**Peacocks** have long tail feathers that reflect different colours as the bird turns. The feathers change from yellow to green to blue. This glittery 'iridescence' helps attract a mate.

# Green grass

Chlorophyll is a green pigment in plants.
It uses light to create food in a process
called photosynthesis. Chlorophyll absorbs
red and blue light, but reflects green
– so nature is painted in shades of green.

The skin of a **lizard** has a different type of green colour. It is camouflaged in a forest of green.

# Blood red

Most animals have red blood. The red pigment carries oxygen, which gives the animal energy. But some animals have blue blood, a few have green, and just one has strange clear blood.

**Squid** have blue blood. The blue pigment is good at picking up the extra oxygen they need to power them through cold water in deep seas.

**Icefish** have ghostly colourless blood without any pigment at all. They lead slow lives in freezing water. They don't use much energy, so they don't need red blood.

**Green-blooded skinks** have a poisonous pigment in their blood. Scientists are still learning how the lizards can live with this deadly poison flowing around their bodies!

# Glow in the dark

Night is dark because there is no light from the Sun. Some animals send messages in the dark by making their own lights. This 'bioluminescence' glows in different colours.

glow-worms

Most night-time glows on land are yellow or green. But the **railroad worm** flicks on its fiery red headlight to warn predators to stay away.

fungi

An **owl** has huge eyes to collect as much light as possible. But it still sees the world in shades of grey because its eyes have mostly rod cells and very few colour-sensitive cone cells.

firefly

# Glossary

**absorb**
To soak up.

**bioluminescence**
Light made by some animals and fungi.

**camouflage**
A way for an animal to hide when its body matches the colour, shape or pattern of its surroundings.

**cells**
The tiny parts that make up all living things.

**gas**
A material like air that is so light that it floats around us and has no fixed shape.

**iridescence**
When colours change as you look at them from different directions.

**light wave**
Light travelling forwards in a wave-like movement.

**mate**
One of a pair of animals that might have babies together. A male animal looks for a female mate.

**nectar**
The sweet liquid inside flowers that bees and birds drink.

**nitrogen**
A see-through gas that has no smell or colour.

**optic nerve**
The optic nerve carries information from the eye to the brain. 'Optic' means 'to do with seeing'. A nerve is a tiny, thin, string-like material that carries messages to and from the brain.

**oxygen**
A see-through gas in the air that many living things need to survive.

**pigment**
A tiny material inside an object or living thing that makes colour.

**predator**
An animal that hunts and eats other animals.

**reflect**
To bounce back light from a surface.

**retina**
A layer of cells that lines the back of the eye. The retina senses light.

**ultraviolet**
Very short light waves that are invisible to humans. Some birds, insects and sea creatures can see ultraviolet light.

**wavelength**
The distance between one high point of a light wave and the next high point.

**white light**
Light that is a mixture of all colours and so looks white. Sunlight is white light.